A NOTE TO PARENTS

When your children are ready to "step into reading," giving them the right books is as crucial as giving them the right food to eat. **Step into Reading Books** present exciting stories and information reinforced with lively, colorful illustrations that make learning to read fun, satisfying, and worthwhile. They are priced so that acquiring an entire library of them is affordable. And they are beginning readers with a difference—they're written on five levels.

Early Step into Reading Books are designed for brand-new readers, with large type and only one or two lines of very simple text per page. **Step 1 Books** feature the same easy-to-read type as the Early Step into Reading Books, but with more words per page. **Step 2 Books** are both longer and slightly more difficult, while **Step 3 Books** introduce readers to paragraphs and fully developed plot lines. **Step 4 Books** offer exciting nonfiction for the increasingly independent reader.

The grade levels assigned to the five steps—preschool through kindergarten for the Early Books, preschool through grade 1 for Step 1, grades 1 through 3 for Step 2, grades 2 through 3 for Step 3, and grades 2 through 4 for Step 4—are intended only as guides. Some children move through all five steps very rapidly; others climb the steps over a period of several years. Either way, these books will help your child "step into reading" in style!

To Kate . . . at last!
And to Heidi . . . for all she has taught me.
And to the Gramblings . . . with special thanks to Art for his extraordinary support on this one.
— L.G.

With love to my mom.
— B.S.T.

Text copyright © 1998 by Lois Grambling. Illustrations copyright © 1998 by Bridget Starr Taylor.
All rights reserved under International and Pan-American Copyright Conventions.
Published in the United States by Random House, Inc., New York, and simultaneously
in Canada by Random House of Canada Limited, Toronto.

Library of Congress Cataloging-in-Publication Data
Grambling, Lois G. Happy Valentine's Day, Miss Hildy! / by Lois Grambling ;
illustrated by Bridget Starr Taylor.
p.   cm.—(Step into reading. Step 2 book)
SUMMARY: Miss Hildy uses her knowledge of spelling to discover the identity of her secret admirer.
ISBN 0-679-88870-5 (pbk.). — ISBN 0-679-98870-X (lib. bdg.) [1. Mystery and detective stories.
2. English language—Spelling—Fiction. 3. Valentine's Day—Fiction.] I. Taylor, Bridget Starr, ill.
II. Title. III. Series. PZ7.G7655Hap 1998 [E]—dc21 97-14041

http://www.randomhouse.com/

Printed in the United States of America 10 9 8 7 6 5 4 3

STEP INTO READING is a registered trademark of Random House, Inc.

Step into Reading®

Happy Valentine's Day, Miss Hildy!

By Lois Grambling
Illustrated by
Bridget Starr Taylor

Be Mine

A Step 2 Book

Random House 🏠 New York

Chapter 1

Miss Hildy was a detective.

At least, *she* thought so.

She had a cape, a cap,

a magnifying glass,

and a little black book for taking notes.

More than anything

(except maybe her cup of afternoon tea),

Miss Hildy loved to solve mysteries.

Today was Valentine's Day.

Miss Hildy had just cracked

the case of "Who Stole Farmer Brown's

Attack Chicken?"

She was resting.

Until her doorbell rang.

Miss Hildy opened the door.

What a surprise!

On her doorstep stood

twelve lovely long-legged flamingos!

"Oh, my!" she said.

"Are you distant relatives

coming to visit?"

she asked.

The flamingos shook their heads.

One of them handed Miss Hildy a card.

Miss Hildy smelled a mystery.

12 LUVLY
VALENTYNES
FOR YOU
FROM A
SECRET ADMIRER

Or maybe it was the flamingos

she smelled.

Either way, Miss Hildy had

a mystery to solve.

Who was her secret admirer?

Chapter 2

Miss Hildy could hardly wait

to get started.

But she wondered

what to do with her flamingos.

Then she had an idea.

Her umbrella stand would

work as a vase.

So she filled it with water

and stood her flamingos in it.

"You remind me of twelve

lovely long-stemmed red roses

I was once given," she said, smiling.

Miss Hildy started searching for clues.

First she examined each flamingo.

Her detective eye found nothing.

Except that many of them had fleas.

"Good thing I put you in water,"

she said, handing them a bar of soap.

"Phew! You all need a bath."

Next Miss Hildy examined the card.

Her detective eye noticed something.

Several words were misspelled.

"Aha!" she said. "A clue!

My secret admirer is a terrible speller.

I will make a list of everyone

who *could* be my secret admirer.

Then I will check their spelling."

Miss Hildy got out her little black book and wrote:

Mr. Truffle?

Lives in Apartment 7

Owns a candy shop

Slips in extra chocolates when I buy a pound

Next on the list was:

Mr. Herring?

Lives in Apartment 11

Owns a fish market

Slips in extra shrimp when I buy a pound

"Oh, dear," Miss Hildy said.

"I have run out of secret admirers.

Unless…"

Miss Hildy wrote down another name.

Mr. Byrd ???

Moved into
Apartment 12

Owns new
shop near
fish market

Carries my
garbage to the
curb for me
every MONDAY

It was time to start detecting.

She put on her cape and her cap.

"Make yourselves at home,"

she said to her valentines as she left.

And did they ever!

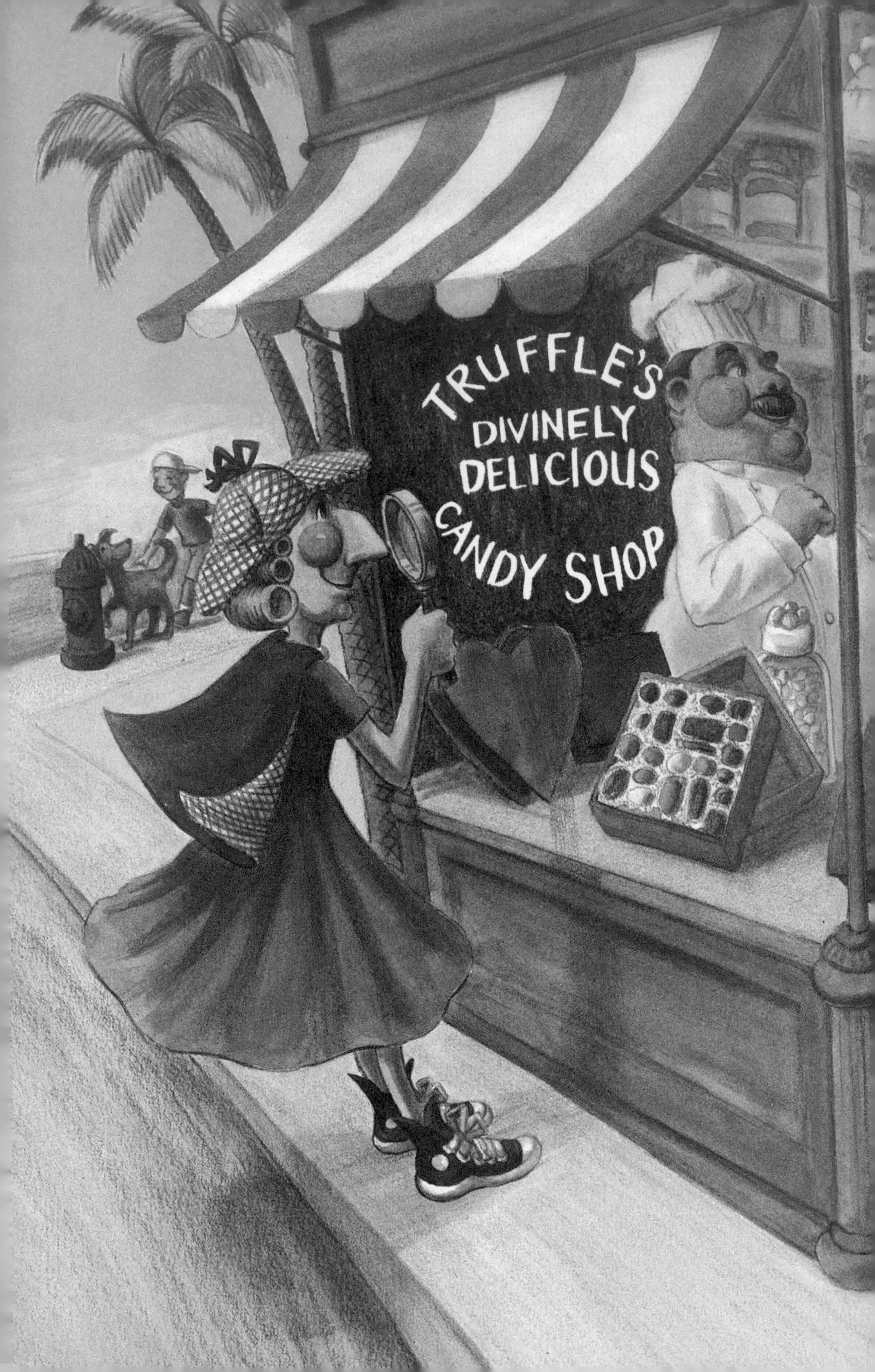
TRUFFLE'S
DIVINELY
DELICIOUS
CANDY SHOP

Chapter 3

Miss Hildy's first stop

was Mr. Truffle's candy shop.

She examined the sign

painted on the window.

Next she examined the small sign

taped to the door.

Valentine
Special
TODAY

Miss Hildy's detective eye
noticed something.

All the words on the signs
were spelled correctly.

"Mr. Truffle is an excellent speller,"
she said.

"He cannot be my secret admirer.
Besides, he probably would have
sent me chocolates."

Miss Hildy crossed Mr. Truffle

off her list.

Her next stop:

Mr. Herring's fish market.

HERRING'S
Delivered Daily
FISH MARKET
Each fish guaranteed
to **SMELL** fresh

Chapter 4

Miss Hildy stood in front

of Herring's fish market.

She examined the sign

hanging in the window.

Next she examined the small sign
taped to the door.

Miss Hildy's detective eye noticed
that not one word was misspelled.

"Mr. Herring also is an excellent speller," she said.

"*He* cannot be my secret admirer. Besides, he probably would have sent me lobsters."

Miss Hildy crossed Mr. Herring off her list.

Miss Hildy began to worry.

She was running out of possible

secret admirers.

Unless…

Miss Hildy's next stop:

Mr. Byrd's new shop.

Chapter 5

Mr. Byrd's new shop was hard to miss.

Two red banners flapped in the breeze.

So did dozens of red balloons.

"Perfect for Valentine's Day,"

Miss Hildy thought.

Miss Hildy examined the sign

hanging in the window.

BYRD'S
XOTIC and
OUT of the ORDINARY
PET SHOP
All pets garenteed
NOT to BYTE

Her detective eye noticed
that many of the words
were misspelled.

Next she examined the small sign
taped to the door.

Miss Hildy's detective eye
popped wide open!
The word "valentine"
was misspelled!

"Mr. Byrd is a terrible speller," she said.
"*He* could be my secret admirer!"

Chapter 6

Miss Hildy hurried into the shop.

"Happy Valentine's Day, Mr. Byrd,"
she said.

"And thank you for sending me
those lovely valentines.
They add a splendid splash of color
to my home."

"Mr. Herring will be pleased
to hear that," said Mr. Byrd.

"Mr. Herring?" said Miss Hildy.
"Owner of the Delivered Daily
Fish Market?"

"That is the one," said Mr. Byrd.

"He asked me to deliver
twelve of my loveliest flamingos
to you."

Miss Hildy opened her little black book.

She guessed her valentine mystery

was about to be solved.

"Let me get the facts straight,"

Miss Hildy said.

"*Mr. Herring* ordered the flamingos?

And *you* delivered them?

And the card that came with them…

You wrote it?

And Mr. Herring told you
what to write?" she asked.
"That is correct," said Mr. Byrd.
Miss Hildy wrote CASE CLOSED
in her little black book.
"Thank you for helping me
crack this case, Mr. Byrd,"
she said.

Chapter 7

Miss Hildy hurried back
to Mr. Herring's fish market.
"Happy Valentine's Day, Mr. Herring,"
she said.
"And thank you for my valentine gift."
Mr. Herring blushed
a deep valentine red.
"You are very welcome, Miss Hildy,"
he said.
"But how did you know *I* sent them?"
"I am a detective," Miss Hildy said.
"It is my job to solve mysteries."
This made Mr. Herring smile.

"Did your detective eye tell you

why I sent flamingos?" he asked.

"*Lovely* long-legged flamingos?"

Miss Hildy's detective eye blinked.

"I do not think it did," she said.

"They remind me of you!"

said Mr. Herring.

Now Miss Hildy blushed.

"How nice of you to say that,"

she said.

Miss Hildy pulled something
out of her cape pocket.
It was a plastic bag filled with water.
Inside swam a blowfish.
"I got this valentine gift for you,"
Miss Hildy said.

She handed Mr. Herring the bag.

Mr. Herring blinked.

"What a handsome fish!" he said.

"I thought so, too," said Miss Hildy.

"It is time for afternoon tea,"
said Miss Hildy.
"Would you join me in my kitchen
for a cup?"
"I would love to,"
said Mr. Herring.
"And please, call me Red."
"And please," said Miss Hildy,
"call me Tildy."

Miss Hildy's kitchen table
was a bit crowded that afternoon.
But no one seemed to mind.

Miss Hildy is still a detective.

At least, *she* thinks so.

But now more than anything

(except maybe solving mysteries),

Miss Hildy loves having her cup

of afternoon tea with Mr. Herring.

And Miss Hildy's flamingos?

They love their new home.

And they *love* the fresh shrimp
Mr. Herring brings them
every afternoon.